Who Stole My Letter?

Who Stole My Letter?

Henry L. Jones

To order additional copies of this book, contact:
HLJ Childrens Stories
1338 Hanley St.
Gary, IN 46404
1-219-951-7529
www.hljchildrensstories.com
Printed by In-Printgraphics
www.in-printgraphics.com

ACKNOWLEDGEMENT
Forward

Over a span of twenty years, I have written stories, poems, and prose in longhand. Now that we are in the digital age, I've found myself struggling to catch up and enter the twenty-first century. I have been encourged by some friends and family. Some transformed my scribbles to digital. Some made critical suggestions and corrections. I am grateful for the support of Dorothy Jones, Helen Comer, Maxine Whiting, Wilma Brown, Bertha Conley and Kee-Kee for encourgement, and help in preparing the script for the digital age.

Henry L. Jones

Chapter One

Miss Carter looked beyond the first row and called on Jerald. Jerald thought for a few seconds. "I want a power ranger, a robot, and a radio controlled car."

Miss Carter was making a list of toys, games, and clothing that her third grade pupils wanted on the board. Her third grade class was going to write letters to Santa Claus.

"That's great, Jerald. We'll list a few more." She called on a couple of students who seldom participate and asked them what they wanted. Some of the pupils wanted the same things; she suggested that they end the list.

Miss Carter reviewed the list of words on the board, the pronunciation, and the spelling of each. Pupils were told that they could choose any of the gifts to include in their letter to Santa. They were instructed to try to make complete sentences as they wrote their letters.

There was great enthusiasm and all were eager to get started. Pencils were sharpened, and the lined paper was provided. Miss Carter then spoke firmly. "Class, let us look at the sample letter on the board." She pointed to the position of the date, the greeting, the body of the letter, and the closing. "Be sure to follow the form of the sample letter and try to space your letters evenly."

The class of nineteen boys and girls were eager to start. When she gave the "ok" to start, nineteen heads bent forward and nineteen pencils danced on the paper. Each had an extra reason for wanting to do a very good job of letter writing. Their letters were going to be placed on the board before Christmas, and five of the best-written letters would be sent to Gregory's, the fanciest department store downtown. The winners would be awarded toys from the department store.

Suddenly, the fire bell rang, bringing their work to an abrupt stop. "Pencils down; line up by rows," Miss Carter spoke in a quiet but firm voice. She grabbed her roll book and headed for the door. "Last pupil out, please close the door," she requested.

With arms folded across their chests, Miss Carter's pupils fell in line behind Mrs. Patterson's class. Once outside the building, they lined up on the playground a safe distance from the school. They were urged to stay in line, to keep their hands folded across their chests, and to be quiet. When the all-clear signal was given, Miss Carter's students began to sigh and comment about finishing their letters. "Quiet, please!" Miss Carter and Mrs. Patterson commanded.

Miss Carter, the first to reach the classroom, advised her pupils to return to their seats and finish their letters. She had not expected any interruptions. She hoped that they could finish before lunch. Her thoughts were interrupted by a sudden outburst. "Where is my letter? Who took my letter?"

The voice told Miss Carter that Carletta Hill was the upset pupil. She closed the door and walked towards Carletta. "Carletta, what is the problem?"

"Somebody took my letter," Carletta stated in a voice that expressed anger and disgust.

"Don't get excited. Look around. It may be on the floor." Miss Carter suggested.

"I looked. It ain't on the floor and it ain't on my desk."

Miss Carter could see that Carletta was upset. This was her first year with this class, and she didn't know quite what to expect. She thought that Carletta was about to cry, but there was anger in her eyes, also. Miss Carter quickly stepped to Carletta's side and put an arm around her shoulder.

"Everyone look around on the floor. Hopefully we will find it." Every pupil in the class now was drawn into the problem, and they were not too pleased. Some made a quick glance around and a few did not. They wanted to finish their letters to Santa. "We had to rush for the fire drill, so it could have fallen on the floor."

Miss Carter was trying to quiet her students. There was a feeling of tension in the air. Carletta, the tallest girl in the class, stood next to Jason's desk. Jason, seated behind Carletta, was a prankster. His face did not always reflect what was going on in his mind.

"Miss Carter, maybe she took her letter with her," Jason shouted.

"Boy!" Carletta injected, "I left my letter on my desk. Why is everybody's on they desk?"

"On 'their' desk, Carletta," Miss Carter whispered.

"I didn't take it." Jason said with a smirk on his face.

"Maybe the Grinch took it." Malcolm said mockingly. The class began laughing. Some laughs were mocking and some were just snickers of amusement. Jason, usually a timid boy, could be mean.

"Class!" Miss Carter called firmly. "This isn't anything to make fun of. Malcolm, your comment was unnecessary. In fact, it was unkind."

"Yes 'sum, sorry." Malcolm said in an under-eyed sheepish tone.

"Miss Carter," Carletta spoke boldly, "you got some thieves in this class."

"Carletta, we don't make statements without proof. There are no 'thieves' in this class. Is that clear?"

"Somebody stole my letter," Carletta said with emphasis.

"Carletta, come up to my desk." She felt the need to ease Carletta's anger and to get the class on track.

"Now I don't have a letter for Santa. Somebody stole my letter."

"Carletta, don't say that! Let's just say your letter is missing."

Carletta mumbled under her breath, but Miss Carter clearly heard. "Somebody stole my letter. Some thieves . . . ."

"Don't! Don't use that word Carletta. That is not nice. Sit down here." She placed a chair next to her desk. Carletta sat down. She was angry. Everybody had a letter but her.

Why was her letter missing? There was only one answer. Somebody stole her letter, and she had to get it back. After Miss Carter directed the class back to their individual letters, she sat down and directed her attention to Carletta. Carletta was still angry. There was a sullen look on her face.

Usually, Carletta was a quiet and pleasant student. Unless she was provoked, she did not draw attention to herself. Her height was the only factor that stood out. For that reason alone, pupils either shied away from her, or, on occasions, made fun of her.

"Carletta, you can start another letter. Would you want to start another?" Miss Carter asked.

"No," Carletta sniffed. "I want the letter I started." She sniffed again. This time the entire class looked up. "Somebody stole my letter!"

Some members of the class wanted to snicker. Some thought it was funny. Many of them turned and smiled to each other. Some felt uneasy. Carletta had said that there were thieves in the class. Her letter was missing. Maybe one or more of the thieves had stolen her letter to Santa. They all sat as if under a cloud—a cloud with the word T-H-I-E-V-E-S written on it. "I wrote a special letter, Miss Carter. I don't care if it 'git' on the board. It was special," she sobbed angrily.

Miss Carter tried to soothe Carletta's feelings. "I'm sure it was a special letter Carletta. I want you to practice writing a letter, so won't you try?"

"Let's try again, ok?" She gave Carletta a tissue to dry her eyes and face. "Sit here for a few minutes; I'll get you a new sheet."

Miss Carter went about the class checking for progress. She checked spelling, spacing, and penmanship. She also checked to see if their sentences were good clear sentences. Many of the pupils were nearly finished.

RIN-N-N-N-G! The lunch bell sounded. "Boys and Girls, sit for a minute. Marcie, collect all letters. Make sure you get a letter from each student. Make sure your name is on your letter."

Carletta dried her eyes, but she was still angry. Her puffed lips and pouty mouth were those of a third grader whose feelings were hurt. And to make matters worse, Miss Carter was collecting the letters, every letter but hers.

Huh! Some rat stole her letter, and she wanted it back. Maybe she would have to find a way to get her letter back. It was a very special, special letter.

After the letters were collected, Miss Carter told Carletta to get ready for lunch. She would talk to her afterwards.

Chapter Two

Miss Carter joined the other teachers in the teachers' lounge. They chatted briefly about how the fire drill interrupted activities.

One teacher noted that the energy was higher when the pupils returned from the drill. The art teacher, Mrs. Atkins, wished that she had a fore warning so that certain things like glue or paints could be sealed.

"Well, my only problem was that one student's letter to Santa could not be found when we returned. She thinks that somebody took her letter. She even labeled somebody a thief."

Some of the teachers thought that was amusing and chuckled mostly a light laugh. "Did she find it?" Mrs. Atkins asked.

"No, I asked my students to look around. No one found it, and it wasn't on the floor."

"We're going to start our letters tomorrow," Mrs. Harris said. She was a third grade teacher, too. "I had a notion that we were due for a drill."

"Whose letter was it?" Miss Booker asked. Miss Booker was a tall slender spinster. She was a veteran second grade teacher. Most of her second grade students were placed in Miss Carter's class, along with Carletta. "It was Carletta's letter."

'OH BOY!" Miss Booker sighed. "I hope you can help her keep her temper under control. She can do good work, but she needs help when it comes to controlling her attitude."

Miss Booker's words were meant to give Miss Carter a clue to helping Carletta overcome an attitude problem. "Did you let her get started on another?"

"Well, the lunch bell rang before I could get her started." Miss Carter felt a twinge of remorse as she spoke.

In the lunchroom, Miss Carter's class was directed to a long table where they sat as a class. The usual lively spirits, the constant chatter, questions about each others lunch, and the laughter were missing. *Was the thief at the table? Who took Carletta's letter?* There was an uneasy feeling among the students. The big question on everyone's mind was: Who was going to sit next to Carletta? Everyone was on edge.

Carletta had openly said that she would choke the thief. When they sat down, Caletta sat beside Macie. "Oh my goodness," Macie thought. "I don't have her letter." Macie was one of the smallest girls in the class. Macie didn't open her lunchbox until Carletta started eating her pizza and fries. While they ate, most of the students focused on their lunches, and others kept their eyes on Carletta.

"You know somebody 'took' my letter, Macie. Do you know who took my letter, Macie?" *Poor Macie . . . she was so nervous.* Carletta's voice was low but firm. "I don't sit by 'you,' Macie quietly said. "I don't know where your letter is." Macie wanted to leave the table, but the lunchroom rules required that she stay with her class.

LaMesha, sitting across from Carletta, was all eyes and ears. She spoke up timidly. "Maybe you could write another."

"I want MY letter; I ain't writing another!" All at the table heard Carletta's voice. "Somebody took my letter!"

"Girl, ain't nobody got your letter. You can't spell anyway." Billy responded to her broad accusation. Billy was not a bully, but he was the toughest boy in the class. Though not as tall as Carletta, he was the second largest boy in the class.

"You sit by me," Carletta said to Billy. "You better not have my letter." "If you got it, you better give it back!"

"Girl, the Grinch got your letter." Billy joked.

"I'm gonna Grinch you!" Carletta angrily responded.

"How's lunch today?" Mr. Wallace asked. Immediately all eyes were fixed on the principal, a tall lanky man who towered over the pupils. "I hope that you're enjoying your lunch," he said as he slowly strolled round the table. All eyes were fixed on Mr. Wallace, and, for a brief moment, all mouths stopped chewing.

What a great opportunity for a scared third grader. While all eyes were on Mr. Wallace, mustard stained fingers slipped a folded sheet of paper into the coat pocket of Wally Johnson.

Mr. Wallace moved on to another table, and Miss Carter's class relaxed. The chatter began and for a brief while, they forgot that 'they' were thieves. That is, until Carletta said aloud . . . "Maybe I ought to tell the Principal somebody stole my letter."

Before she could get up, one of the lunchroom matrons reminded then to leave their areas clean, don't forget their coats, and get ready to go outside.

"Great!" Wally thought to himself as he hurriedly cleared his area and put on his coat. Usually, he finished before the others and headed for the playground.

For some very personal reason, Wally enjoyed being the first to arrive on the basketball court. But Wally came to a sudden stop when he excitedly put his hands in his coat pocket. He was near the door that opened to the playground, but he could not move. *He didn't remember having any paper in his pocket.* He pulled out the folded piece of paper and there written on the front CARLETTA HILL.

"*No way! I ain't no thief,*" Wally thought. He was nowhere near Carletta in the cafeteria or in the classroom. The best thing to do, he thought, was to slip the letter into somebody else's book or coat. That's what somebody did to him.

Wally went back to the lunch table and struck up a conversation with a few of the other boys in his class. Wally briefly talked about basketball and bragged about his ability to dribble with his left hand. Before he left, his ketchup stained fingers had placed the folded letter in Marcus's book bag.

Miss Carter tried to eat her lunch in some peace, but she couldn't relax her mind nor could the advice of the teachers ease her frustration.

"Well, Carletta can be stubborn. I dealt with her last year. Her mother was positive for the most part. Carletta is her only child, so she can be a bit stubborn, or mean at times."

During the play period, Carletta continued to express her feelings to everyone about her missing letter. She walked up to them one by one and asked in a firm voice "Did you take my letter?" or "Did you steal my letter?" Most of the girls were either jumping rope or swinging and unanimously responded "NO." The other girls would give Carletta the same attitude she gave them, "Girl—No, I ain't seen yo letter, and I ain't no thief!"

When Carletta asked little Macie Simmons, Macie appeared to shrink. She was the smallest and shortest in the class. She simply shook her head from left to right and uttered "unh-unh' and took off running.

In the teacher's lunchroom, Miss Booker, realizing that Miss Carter was the new teacher, wanted to provide insight into Carletta's problem.

"I never met her father. He is in the army. I know that her mother works at the hospital. She was able to come to school two or three times last year.

She told me that she would come more often, but her job wouldn't allow her the time she needed. She wants Carletta to do well, but she has to get Carletta's aunt to help her out. Carletta goes—I guess she goes to her aunt's after school. Have you talked with Carletta's aunt yet?"

"No," Miss Carter answered. *The lunch bell sounded.* "I guess I'll try after school."

When the bell rang, signaling the end of lunch, Miss Carter's class lined up and returned quietly to class. There was not the casual cheerful exchanges and excitement. Carletta had cast a cloud of suspicion over everyone.

As the class entered the room, Brianna hurried over to Miss Carter. "What is it, Brianna?"

"Miss Carter, Carletta's been calling people a thief. She's been asking who took her letter." Brianna dashed back to her desk.

"Oh, my goodness," Miss Carter thought. "Am I going to get through this afternoon? Do I search each desk, every book bag, or every coat pocket?"

The schedule called for a review of math problems, and then there would be a practice session for the Christmas musical.

She had planned to check over the letters while the class was with the music teacher. But with Brianna's message, she could not be sure. Using a raised palm, Miss Carter urged her class to be seated and to take out their math books.

"Miss Carter!" Shelby called out, "Carletta been asking about her letter!"

"I know, Shelby," she replied in a firm voice. She really didn't want to deal with the letter at this time.

"Miss Carter, did you get my letter?" Carletta asked in an anxious tone.

"No, Carletta, no one turned it in."

"Did you look, Miss Carter?" Her voice was one pleading and anxious. "Could you look?"

"OH Heaven Help Me!" Miss Carter pleaded silently.

"Carletta, please be patient. I told you that you could write a new letter."

"My letter was special." Carletta looked at her classmates. Her jaws were firm, her lips were drawn, and her eyes were squinted. "Somebody took my letter."

"Not me!" Shelby exclaimed.

"Me neither," Rosa said flatly.

"I ain't seen it," Robert chimed.

A chorus of "I didn't do it" and "I ain't seen it" flowed out in disharmony.

"Help me! P-L-E-A-S-E!" Miss Carter begged silently.

"Miss Carter, I know who got her letter," Billy said with a straight face, "Rudolph the Red Nosed Reindeer." He kept a straight face, but the class roared with laughter.

"Class . . . Class! That's not funny. Quiet everyone!" She looked at Billy sternly. "Billy, would you like for your letter to disappear? Would you like for your letter not to be sent to the department store? Would you want to miss out on an opportunity to win some toys?"

Billy answered with a soft, "No."

"Then be quiet. Learn to be kind to others. I don't know what happened to Carletta's letter, and I'm sorry. But, we all know that she can write 'another' letter—Right Carletta?" Miss Carter smiled, looked, and nodded at Carletta.

Miss Carter's words didn't help. Carletta was angry, but quiet.

"She called us a thief, Miss Carter."

"Raymond! Please! You know there are no thieves in the room, and your comment is upsetting to Carletta. When people are upset, they make mistakes. So let's not make any more mistakes. Not unless you want a few demerits for bad jokes, name calling, or not getting your math books out."

At that, all math books came out and pages began to turn. Carletta, zombie-like, followed in slow motion.

After math, several class members went to the cafeteria. They were practicing for the Christmas play. All the others were allowed to work on their letters. Carletta faked working. She was still angry and could not focus on another letter.

Chapter Three

At Kenny's Home

"Grandma—guess what?" Kenny was bursting. He had to tell his grandmother that he had been called a thief. "This girl in class called everybody a thief."

"Why?" His grandmother was busy preparing supper. "Why would she do that?"

"See, we had to write a letter to Santa Claus. But the bell for the fire drill rang. We had to go out. When we got back in class, her letter was missing. So she said a thief took it."

"Well, you didn't take it, did you?"

"No!"

"Well, you're not a thief, but 'somebody' in the class is. Don't you ever steal anything! A thief is one of the lowest beings on earth."

At Marcus's Home

Marcus's mother was a very energetic slender woman. She was very active in school and in the church. She was rushing Marcus to get a snack so they could go to a meeting at church.

"Ma, guess what?"

"What, Marcus?"

"This girl Carletta, she asked me if I stole her letter.

"I told her, NO! I didn't steal her letter."

"Why would she ask you?"

"All during lunch hour she was asking everyone in the class if they stole her letter to Santa."

"I don't understand, Marcus. When did the letter come up missing?"

"Well, Ma, see we had to write a letter to Santa, but the fire bell rang, and we had to go out. When we got back, her letter was gone."

"Was it on the floor/"

"No."

"Well, may be that somebody took it," his mother said softly. "Why would somebody steal a letter to Santa? The last place you need a thief is in the classroom."

At Gerald's Home

When Gerald emptied his book bag and put his homework on the table, his sister told him, "Boy pick up that piece of paper off the floor."

"What paper?" Gerald asked as he looked down.

"You see that folded up piece of paper. You act like you scared to pick it up."

Celia, his sister, had to sweep the kitchen. She certainly did not want to have extra trash put on the floor.

Gerald froze for a brief period. "What is that?" he thought. "Could it be—no—It couldn't be Carletta's letter." He reached down and gingerly picked up the folded piece of paper.

"Whew!" It wasn't Carletta's letter. It was his spelling list.

"I'm glad it wasn't her letter." He said in a low voice.

"Whose letter?" his sister asked.

"This girl in class, she says that somebody took her letter she wrote to Santa Claus. When we came back from the fire drill she couldn't find her letter."

"So you thought that piece of paper was her letter? Boy, are you sure you ain't no thief? You sure you didn't take her letter?"

"Girl!" Gerald said in a high voice, "I don't steal. Why would I take somebody's letter?"

"You always take my things. You steal at home. You steal at school." She teased.

Their mother interrupted them.

"Who steals what?" She queried in a serious tone.

"Nothing, Ma," Gerald responded quickly. "Mama, this girl, you know Carletta lives down the block. Well, somebody took her letter that she wrote to Santa. We couldn't find it after the fire drill. Now, she won't have a letter on the board or one to go to the store where Santa will be."

"Can't she write another letter?" his mother asked.

"I guess so. But she thinks somebody stole her letter, and she acting like she ready to beat somebody up."

"You just make sure that you didn't take her letter. I don't raise thieves in my house."

At Carletta's Home

Down the block, Carletta was expressing her anger and dislike for her classmates. Somebody stole her letter, and, yes, she felt like crying. She also felt like she could squeeze the neck of the thief until he cried for mercy. Somehow, she felt like blaming the teacher.

"You shouldn't blame the teacher," her mother said. Carletta's mother worked each day at a residence for elderly people. She was a hard working woman who cared for everything in her home.

"But, Mama, she took up everybody's letter but mine," Carletta spoke with emphasis. "She didn't make them look in their desks or nothing. I just know that one of them thieves took my letter. Now, I won't have a letter to enter in the contest."

"Don't worry, Carletta, I'll write your teacher a note and ask if you can write another letter to Santa."

Carletta didn't respond. Her letter was a special letter, with a special request. She wanted that letter back.

Later that evening, Marcus and his mother went to church. His mother was meeting with the church's Mission Club. Marcus and a few other children were allowed to use a separate room to study in.

Marcus sat at one end of a table and two other boys sat at the far end. He knew those boys. They went to school with Marcus. But they weren't in his class. They were in Mrs. Harris's class. Mrs. Harris hadn't assigned any homework, so they admired each others basketball card collection and comic books.

Marcus had spelling words to study and some math problems to solve. First, he took out his sandwich, a small carton containing a fruit juice. "Yummy, yum, yum," he thought as he unwrapped the peanut butter and jelly sandwich. The snack would satisfy his hunger until they got home.

When he finished his snack, he hurriedly wiped his mouth with the wax paper from his sandwich. He threw the paper in the trash, grabbed his book bag and began pulling out paper.

"What?" he thought as he pulled out an unfamiliar piece of folded paper. "What is this?"

It took only a few seconds for Marcus to realize that he had forbidden property. "Oh-h No—this ain't the letter!" he said aloud. The two students at the far end of the table looked up in surprise.

"What's up?" one of the boys asked.

Marcus couldn't answer for a minute. His eyes were focused on the name Carletta Hill. "No-o-o, this ain't mine. I brought the wrong homework," he finally replied. "Wow." What could he do? He thought about putting the letter in the trash. The curious boys may get nosey. If the boys gave the letter to Carletta, he would be accused of stealing her letter.

Well, there was just one thing to do. Folding the letter carefully with his jelly-stained hands, he put it in a pocket of his book bag. He would simply slip it in a friend's book bag. He even decided which friend's bag he would put it in.

Chapter Four

Pupils who arrive at school early are allowed to enter the gym when the weather is bad. Marcus couldn't have planned it any better . . . a crowded gym. And, to top it off, his "friend/victim" had placed his book bag down to go get a drink of water.

As Gerald neared the fountain, Marcus put the jelly-ketchup-mustard stained folded paper in Gerald's bag. He breathed a sigh of relief, and yet, he had an uneasy feeling. Being a thief was not part of his character. He was a mischievous fellow at times, but, a thief . . . No Way! It wasn't easy for him to smile and joke with Gerald when he came back.

Marcus felt better when they left the gym and went to class. He felt like he'd shed a problem. It was not his problem now. Gerald, who sat near Carletta, would have to deal with "the letter."

After the usual opening, recitation of the pledge and the singing of "America the Beautiful," Miss Carter reviewed the schedule for the morning. She did not mention the Christmas letter project. She'd do that later. Frankly, she didn't want to think about that until the other class work was done.

Her plan went well until it was time to engage the class in their dictionary drill and spelling work. Gerald began taking books, notebook, and papers out of his book bag. Some papers fell to the floor. He opened each folded sheet to check it before returning it to his book bag.

The first sheet was his math homework. The second sheet was *fatal!* CARLETTA'S LETTER!! Gerald's eyes widened. He stopped breathing for a few seconds. He couldn't believe his eyes. He was afraid to ball the letter up and throw it away. As Gerald attempted to take out the last sheet from his book bag, Billy Sims asked, "Is that Carletta's letter?"

Everybody in the class looked at Billy, then at Gerald. Gerald's eyes widened and his mouth dropped. Then a smile came over his face. He got up and walked toward Miss Carter. Miss Carter was half way to Gerald's desk when he handed her his math homework.

"Billy." Miss Carter said firmly, you remain in class when the lunch bell rings. Don't get out of your seat." Miss Carter's mood changed from that of a pleasant teacher to that of a firm disciplinarian. She had hoped that the "letter" would not be an issue, but to her surprise Carletta came forward with an envelope.

"Miss Carter, I forgot to give you this letter from my mother." Gerald returned to his desk with a sly grin on his face. He would not be known as the thief. Besides, Carletta could be a mean, mean sister. He wanted no part of Carletta. Carletta sat down.

As Carletta sat down, the eyes of most of her class members followed her. Billy was a bit upset having to stay in class longer, so he spoke up, Miss Carter."

"Yes, Billy."

"How long do I got to stay in? Didn't you get Carletta's letter from Gerald?"

"For your information, he turned in his homework. And for everyone's good, take out your homework. We will check it before the lunch hour begins." She placed Carletta's letter in her planning book. It would occupy part of her lunch hour.

Miss Carter began reviewing and checking the homework. She called different class members to work the problems on the chalkboard.

Before the lunch bell rang, Billy was given the task of collecting the math homework and taking the wastebasket around so that scrap paper could be collected.

What a break! Gerald realized he could ditch the letter, and he did just that. He slid the letter under the book that Billy left on his desk. Just before she excused the class for lunch, Miss carter called Carletta to her desk. She promised to send a reply to her mother and discuss the letter during the afternoon.

After the class was dismissed, Miss Carter turned to Billy. He had a sour look on his lean brown face. "Miss Carter." He called. "How long do I have to stay in?"

"Until." She replied in a firm voice.

"Until!" He said in an anxious voice. "Until when, Miss Carter?"

"Until you write a letter apologizing to Carletta for joking about the letter and also for being an antagonist."

"A who?"

"A troublemaker, Billy. Now get out a sheet of paper and write a letter of apology."

"How do you spell apology?"

"Sound it out. Get a dictionary, sound it out. A-P-O-L-O-G-Y. Now get busy if you want to go to lunch."

While Billy was spending an extra ten minutes in class, she would read the letter that Carletta's mother wrote. Writing the letter might have been easy if he hadn't moved the math book. When he unfolded the piece of paper and saw Carletta's heading, his mouth flew open, and he gasped for air.

"Is something wrong, Billy?" Billy sucked in air and stammered, "N-N-No. I need some paper."

"Get a sheet; you know where the paper is kept."

Billy shoved the "letter" back under his math book. He feared Miss Carter would see it because he sat near the teacher's desk.

Now he was in a terrible spot. He was puzzled. How in the world did her letter get beneath his book? Clearly somebody did this dirty trick. They were trying to get him in trouble.

Billy's mind was racing. *"If Miss Carter knew that I had the 'letter,' I would not only be accused of joking about it, but also stealing and hiding it. NO-WAY,"* he thought. NO WAY was he going to keep this letter. He knew that he had to get rid of it. Maybe if he hurried, up, he could slip it to somebody else. He hurried to finish his letter. Miss Carter took the letter and gave him a late pass to the lunch room.

Billy rushed to the lunchroom. Miss Carter found the teachers in the lounge discussing the Christmas program that was coming up soon. "What kept you, Miss Carter?" Ms. Booker asked. "Did my dear Carletta stir up things today?"

"No-o-o. I did get a note from her mother. She wants Carletta to write another, but Carletta doesn't seem to want to. She wants 'that' letter. I guess it is a special letter as she says."

"Well, maybe she doesn't want to start over. She is the only one who has to do it over," Mrs. Atkins reasoned out loud.

"Well, it's not Carletta so much as it is the jokesters, like Billy, who keep making comments about it. Their wisecracks keep Carletta stirred up. So today I kept him in the class after the bell rang so that he could write a letter of apology."

"Good," Miss Booker chimed in. "That Billy is a problem. You have to keep ahead of him."

"I certainly do," Miss Carter said exhaustedly. Their conversation reverted to the Christmas program.

Back in the lunchroom, most of Billy's classmates were almost done with their lunches when he hastily sat down by LaMesha. He took out a sandwich and a fruit drink. "Gosh!" he exclaimed. "I got here late. I wanted to get some fries. Do you want some fries, LaMesha? I'll buy 'em; you go get 'em, okay?"

"Ok." LaMesha eagerly took the coins and hurried to get the fries. When she returned, they split the fries.

"Did you write your apology?" she asked.

"Yeah."

"She's gonna make you read it. You watch."

"I don't care."

In a short time the lunch matron announces, "Time to clear out. Finish your lunch. Everybody to the gym. It's raining. Everybody go to the gym."

When they left the lunchroom, LaMesha went to the restroom. It was there that she discovered the "letter" in her pocket. "Oh, my gosh!" she thought. "That Billy set me up." Like the others who found the letter, she didn't read it. Just the recognition of the name caused panic. "I ain't no thief, and I didn't steal this letter, and I'm gonna give it back."

She looked for Billy during the remainder of the lunch hour. She could not find him in the gym. Billy wisely stood just outside the exit doors. Fortunately the rain had stopped. LaMesha's problem had to be solved soon. She was standing in line with the students to head back to class. She needed an opportunity or a ploy. She looked down the line of students behind her and then those in front. She was searching for a pocket, a bag, or someone.

Suddenly, the shuffling students stopped moving forward. A pushing match started. Students began stumbling back and forth. LaMesha forcefully pushed forward. She arrived at the focal point. Her friend Tonya and a fourth grader were arguing.

Just before two teachers arrived, LaMesha stepped between them and wrapped herself around Tonya. She shoved Tonya in another direction as the teachers urged the students to move on to class.

LaMesha and Tonya made a quick dash to the restroom so Tonya could rearrange her hair and clothes. LaMesha held Tonya's coat. It gave LaMesha her chance.

Chapter Five

Before class began that afternoon, Miss carter explained to the class that Billy had a matter to take care of, and that she'd check the letters to Santa for spelling and alignment. All would need to be rewritten so that they could be displayed for the parents' visitation. After that, they would be sent to a department store downtown. Immediately, each pupil felt a bit uneasy. Writing a letter to Santa should be an enjoyable learning experience. Instead, there were blank stares on some faces. Others looked worried, especially those who had found the "letter."

LaMesha could not look up. She felt nervous. She wanted to go to the restroom.

"Miss Carter, can I go to the bathroom?"

"No, you just came in from lunch, LaMesha." Miss Carter answered.

Miss Carter could sense the tension in the room, and she tried not to look in Carletta's direction. She would talk to Carletta after the math lesson. "Ok, Billy, it's your time. Your letter of apology is on my desk."

Billy dragged his way to her desk. She gave Billy the letter and directed him to stand in front of the class.

"Do you understand why you're doing this Billy?" she asked.

"Yes ma'm."

"Why?"

"Because I did not speak right," Billy mumbled.

"What you did was not proper. You thought it was funny. It was done to embarrass and to hurt feelings." A quick glance at Carletta showed that her feelings were hurt. Carletta's brow was furrowed, her eyelids narrow, and her face was not very pleasant.

"Ok, Billy. Read your letter." Billy began.

```
Dear Classmates,

        I apologize for speaking out
in class. I am sorry if I caused
bad feelings.

                        Your Classmate,
                          Billy Sims
```

"Thank you Billy! Give me your letter. Take your seat. We need to check our math practice sheets. Let's get them ready."

"You took mine before lunch." Billy volunteered.

It was during the practice session that Tonya reached into her jacket pocket to get a tissue for her tearing eyes. What she felt was a sticky, folded sheet of paper with chocolate, mustard, ketchup, and jelly stains.

"What in the world?" Her eyes enlarged. Her lower jaw dropped. She didn't dare open the sheet fully. "Oh boy," she thought. Her mind could not focus on the math lesson. For the rest of the period, she plotted and schemed. She had to come up with some way to get the "letter" out of her hands. The "letter" was now like a plague. It was like a curse. Nobody wanted to be near Carletta now.

And now, who could admit to even seeing the "letter." If she got up to throw it away, Miss Carter might see her. She would find a way, any kind of way to get the "letter" out of her hand. She would not be accused of stealing Carletta's letter. "I ain't no thief," she said to herself. "Ah," she thought "I should give it to Billy with his smart mouth."

After the math exercise, Miss Carter asked Billy to collect and sharpen pencils before they began to re-write their letters. "Miss Carter!" Carletta cried out, "Did anyone turn in my letter?"

A clap of thunder couldn't have silenced the class more than her question. Those who had seen and possessed her letter breathed nervously. Those who had not were stunned by the question and couldn't believe she was still holding on to the notion that someone stole her letter.

"No, Carletta, but you'll have a chance to write another letter. Please take a seat at my desk, and we'll talk about it."

"Miss Carter, may I pass out the letters?" Tonya asked.

"Yes, here they are." She handed the papers to Tonya. Tonya's left hand was in her pocket as she used her right hand to take the papers from Miss Carter. While Billy quietly sharpened pencils, Miss Carter urged the pupils to look at the corrections they need to make.

"Karen," Miss Carter called, "will you pass out the paper?" Karen passed paper; Billy sharpened pencils; Tonya moved around the room to the other students. Quickly and quietly she slipped the "letter" under Billy's math book. With a sigh of relief, she moved on.

Carletta pulled a chair up to Miss Carter's desk. Miss Carter had read the letter written by Carletta's mother. She was concerned that someone had taken Carletta's letter, and she asked if Carletta would be allowed to write another letter. "You do want to write another, don't you?"

"No!" Carletta's response was soft but firm.

"Why not, Carletta?"

"My letter was special. Whoever took my letter took a 'very' special letter. I want my letter."

Miss Carter could see the seriousness in Carletta's eyes, and she hoped that Carletta would move past the anger and the hurt. Why would this letter cause so much disharmony? Why couldn't Carletta write another letter? What happened to the letter was a mystery.

"Carletta, I don't understand. Your mother wants you to write another letter. She's expecting you to. Don't you want to have one on the board when the parents come next week?"

Carletta stood motionless and silent for a few seconds. Then she spoke in a soft, deliberate tone. "Somebody took my letter. Somebody stole my letter. Miss Carter, you got a thief in here."

"Carletta, no, we don't have a thief in here. We don't know what happened. Sometimes things happen, and we can't explain it. But your mother wants you to write another letter . . . I would like for you to write another letter. I want to see your letter on the board. Don't you?"

Without warning, Carletta's eyes began to tear up. Her face lost its pouty expression. Miss Carter quickly reached for a tissue. She gave it to Carletta. Her sobbing attracted much attention.

Miss Carter urged the class to complete their work before the school day ended. "We need to get our display board ready, so work quietly and finish."

Miss Carter knew that Carletta would not write a letter today. "Carletta," she spoke softly, "Don't try to write today. Sit here; I'll be back." Miss Carter moved about the class checking on the progress of the letter writing.

The attention Carletta's crying got from most of the class was a good thing for Billy. He discovered the dreaded letter under his math book. He looked around at LaMesha. She was the culprit. "Little sneaky one," he thought. Then he realized that LaMesha didn't get up to pass out anything. "Tonya and Karen were walking around the class. "Which one was it?" he contemplated. How could he get rid of it now? Who would get the letter?

When the bell rang and they were lining up to go home, Billy eased the letter in Robert's coat pocket. WHAT A RELIEF! But Billy was still puzzled. Who put the letter back on his desk? Was someone trying to set him up? He knew that he would have to be careful. Billy promised himself that from now until the Holiday break, that letter would not come back to him.

Chapter Six

Robert's mother was a very active member of the women's community program. She often had a meeting at their home. As a single mom, she made certain that she kept Robert engaged in as many activities as the day would allow. She made sure he attended Sunday school, helped with the food giveaway, practiced his trumpet one hour a day, and rehearsed with the children's choir on Saturdays. This would definitely keep him busy and out of trouble.

At the dinner table, Robert began working on his homework. "Ma!" he called. "Ma, can I have some of the fried chicken in the refrigerator?"

"Yes, but don't leave the chicken out."

As he hurriedly chomped down on the fried chicken, some of the crumbs fell on the table. He had a napkin on the table, but wiped his hands on the bottom of his shirt. With a piece of chicken in his left hand, he took the spelling words out of his folder.

Robert reached for the pencil on the table, but noticed that it was worn down. He turned to get another pencil out of his coat pocket. There was no pencil in his pocket; instead, he pulled out a folded piece of paper. When he saw the name Carletta, he got nervous. More than that, he was scared. He began talking to himself. "I didn't take Carletta's letter. I'm no thief. Who put this in my pocket?"

His grease and crumb stained fingers were imprinted on the back and front of the letter. He was so nervous that he went to his mother's room. She was sitting in her recliner resting. He was unsure about what he was going to say to her.

"Ma, you know that girl I told you about who got her letter stolen." "Well . . ."

"You didn't steal it, did you?" his mother asked in a stern voice.

"No, but . . ."

"Well, if you didn't take it Robert, what's the story?"

Robert was speechless now. He couldn't admit that he had the letter in his hand. He knew that he would not get the answer or advice he needed. He mustered up a response. "Oh, she may get to do her letter over."

"Uh huh." Was his mother's response. She was resting, and Robert knew what that meant when she was in her recliner. He would have to solve this problem by himself. By morning, he'd find a way to place the "letter" in somebody's coat, book bag, folder, or book.

Wednesday morning came. It brought a surprise for one student Macie, the smallest, quietest, and most timid girl in the class. Macie found an envelope on her desk with her name on it. From all appearances it was a Christmas card. MERRY CHRISTMAS to Macie was written on the envelope. She was afraid to open it because no one in the class had given her anything before. Her classmates were nosey and not always kind. She quietly put the envelope in her book bag. She would open it later.

A part of the morning was given over to decorating the board on which their letters would go. Christmas was two weeks away. On Friday parents would come and visit classrooms. Everybody would have a letter on the board; everyone except Carletta.

When the lunch bell rang Macie folded the envelope and put it in her jean pocket. She marched along with her class to the cafeteria. She knew that the class would be nosey and wonder why she received a Christmas card so early. The class was to make cards next week. When they reached the cafeteria, Macie asked the matron if she could go to the restroom. Macie hurried to open the envelope. For a moment her mind went blank. "No! This ain't no Christmas card!" She carefully unfolded the dingy soiled piece of paper. She felt her knees tremble. For a brief moment she felt as if she were not in her own body.

Who put this letter on her desk? Who and why? Maybe this person wanted Macie to get in trouble or maybe somebody wanted Carletta to "get her." Her palms were getting sweaty. Macie was too scared to read the letter. She hastily put the letter back in the envelope and in her pocket. She would not take it to Miss Carter, take it home, nor give it to anybody in her class. She needed to hurry back to the lunchroom. But, before she did, she had a mission to carry out.

The school secretary was busy typing on her computer. She looked up to see a tiny student with a hood covering the head and much of the face. As she looked up, the pupil placed an envelope on the desk and said, "This is for the principal." The pupil quickly turned and fled the office.

The secretary wondered if the pupil was a girl or boy. She penciled a note to the principal and carried both to his desk. She taped the note to the envelope and laid them where he could not miss seeing them. She chuckled as she thought about the hooded bearer of the envelope.

When every pupil returned to Miss Carter's class after lunch, there was a range of emotions. Some were uneasy about finding unwanted paper on, around, or in their desks. Ronald and Reginald made sure that there was no strange looking paper on, in, or around their desks.

"What is with you two? Ronald and Reginald, sit down. What are you looking for?"

"They're looking for that 'letter,'" Billy said in a low voice. Some pupils heard him and began laughing.

"Class, there's nothing funny. Sit down please." The laughter ceased, but others were now uneasy. "Where is that letter?" they wondered. Those who had not come in possession of it had heard rumors that several people had seen or knew who'd seen it. No one wanted to be associated with it.

When Mr. Wallace returned to his office, he was met by the secretary who was smiling. "You had a hooded visitor."

"A who?" he was puzzled.

"A hooded visitor, a little person came in the office with a hood covering the head and face and handed me an envelope."

"Was it a girl or a boy?" he asked.

"Mr. Wallace, I couldn't see the face," she said with a bit of laughter.

"I don't know why this pupil took so much to avoid recognition, but like I said, a child covered by a hood left something for you."

Mr. Wallace chuckled, "O-o-K, I'll take a look." Mr. Wallace put away his coat and hat. He read the secretary's note, looked at the writing on the envelope and chuckled. He then pulled out the soiled folded sheet. He began to laugh. The secretary looked up. "Must be a funny letter." She thought.

Mr. Wallace called the secretary to come in his office. He held the much-stained letter out for her to see.

"Looks like a well-traveled letter, doesn't it?" he asked. He thought to himself, "This is the missing letter I've heard about."

"From the looks of it, looks as if everyone was eating when they received it." the secretary commented. "Why did this mystery pupil bring it in?" she asked.

"Well, it's addressed to Macie. I think she's in Miss Carter's class. The letter belongs to Carletta, who is in Miss Carter's class. Will you ask Miss Carter to confer with me during her planning period?"

"I sure will," she said and left. Mr. Wallace sat down and carefully held up the letter to the light. The light, filtering through the paper highlighted numerous soiled fingerprints. From the size and number of fingerprints, he guessed that five to eight people handled the letter.

He then held the letter so that he could read it. It was not the typical third grade letter to Santa. The letter read:

> Dear Santa Claus,
>
> I want you to bring my daddy home for Christmas. I miss my daddy. My mommy cry for him. My mommy is scared when people get blowed up. Please bring my daddy home. He is in the army and my mommy cries and prays for him every night.
>
> Your friend,
> Carletta

"Now, I see why Carletta wants this letter. It certainly is not the typical letter," he thought to himself. He called the secretary back to his office.

"This is Carletta's letter. Take a look."

Carletta's letter moved the secretary. "She really has a good request. But why did our mystery student bring it to you incognito?"

"I learned of the letter missing a few days ago. A couple of students told me about the letter in the cafeteria. It disappeared after the fire drill. I guess Carletta accused someone of being a thief, and maybe they felt intimidated. Apparently, the letter has traveled around."

"Yes, from the finger prints and the stains, I think that this letter has traveled around."

"I really think that Carletta has a genuine request. She's not asking for toys and dolls. She's really writing about a family concern. Be sure to ask Miss Carter to come to the office during her planning period." The secretary smiled and returned to her desk.

Mr. Wallace reread Carletta's letter. He began thinking of a way to make Carletta's search for the special letter and special request end on a positive note.

Miss Carter finished checking some students' papers and placed them back in the grade book. She locked the classroom door and headed to Mr. Wallace's office. She couldn't imagine why he wanted to meet with her. As a new teacher, it could be anyone of several reasons.

She got a friendly smile from the secretary who welcomed her and ushered her to the principal's office. Mr. Wallace, smiling, offered her a seat. She was relaxed, but a bit nervous. She asked, "Is this a meeting concerning any problems? May I ask?"

"Do you have a student named Macie?"

"Yes, I do."

"I know Carletta's in your room, also," he stated. With a broad smile on his face, Mr. Wallace handed over the letter. "Here is your missing letter."

He chuckled as she gingerly reached for the soiled piece of paper. There was a questioning look on her face as she took the letter. She immediately recognized the name and the handwriting.

Mr. Wallace watched the expressions on Miss Carter's face. The puzzled look faded to a relaxed and pleasant expression. "Well, this is Carletta's letter. I can see why she calls it a special letter. How did you get it?"

He gave Miss Carter the envelope addressed MERRY CHRISTMAS to Macie. "I know this handwriting." she said, "It is not Macie's."

"I suspect, since it's addressed to Macie, somebody probably" he paused—"either that person gave it to her or just slipped it on her desk."

They chuckled.

"Mr. Wallace, this has been a perplexing mystery. This letter has caused some bad attitudes and hurt feelings."

"What's the story? How did all this start?"

"Well, it started the day we had our last fire drill. The students were writing letters to Santa. The fire bell rang. The letters were left on their desks. When we returned Carletta's letter was missing. She accused "somebody" of stealing her letter, and it's been a testy, trying situation. Some of the boys have been joking about it. I'm told Carletta's been—well, I guess, intimidating the students, asking questions or accusing classmates."

Mr. Wallace chuckled again. "You know what—the fire drill was Monday. Today is Thursday. Look at the fingerprints. It's gotten around, wouldn't you agree? If each print represents a different pupil, then that letter has been through a lot of hands."

"Do you think that they openly passed her letter around?"

"No, the secretary told me that the pupil who brought it to the office had a hood covering the head and face. She didn't know if it was a girl or boy."

"Oh, my" Miss Carter sighed. "What do you think I should do? The letter is addressed to Santa, but the request is not for toys and gifts. It's really a serious appeal."

"Well, let me think on it. Let me keep her letter for the time being. I'll get with you in a day or so. I'm really struck by her request."

"At least we now know where the letter is and don't have to worry about it traveling about getting more jelly, grease, mustard, ketchup, or chocolate on it," Miss Carter said as she examined the letter.

Mr. Wallace thanked Miss Carter and stated, "We'll talk again on this matter. In the meantime, will you assure Carletta that Santa will get her letter?"

After Miss Carter left the principal's office, Mr. Wallace reached for the telephone book and began working on a plan.

Chapter Seven

Friday was the first day for all groups to practice for the Christmas program. It was also the day that parents have a chance to visit the school and talk to the teacher. Two more weeks and school would be out for the Christmas holiday.

Miss Carter's class was busy decorating the room. They were making red, white, and green loops for paper chains. Their letters had been finished and were ready to go on the board. The only letter not ready was Carletta's. She always managed to pretend that she would finish her letter.

Miss Carter, after finishing talking with Mr. Wallace, decided to leave a space on the board for her letter. After all, it was a special letter. To their surprise, a request came over the intercom. It was the principal's voice. He wanted Carletta to come to the office.

Carletta was nervous. She hadn't been in trouble—especially the kind that caused you to go to the principal's office. She'd been on punishment by Miss Booker, but not by Mr. Wallace.

"Carletta, how are you?" Mr. Wallace warmly greeted her. "Have a seat." She sat down with her eyes fixed on Mr. Wallace. She was puzzled. She had done nothing—not anything serious. Surely, her remark about choking somebody wasn't a direct threat to anyone in particular.

"What did I do, Mr. Wallace?"

"You wrote a letter to Santa, didn't you?"

"Somebody stole it," she quickly replied.

Mr. Wallace smiled. "Made you angry, didn't it?"

"Yes," she said softly. She felt as if Mr. Wallace wanted her to confess to something.

"Somebody stole my letter," she said, trying to muster up a firm voice.

Mr. Wallace continued smiling. "Miss Carter says that your letter is special, right?"

"Yes, Sir, it was special—to me—and, my mother."

"What makes it special, Carletta?"

"I want to see my daddy. My mother wants to see my daddy."

"Where is your dad?"

"He's over there fighting," she held back tears. "My mother worries all the time."

Mr. Wallace could see that she was sincere. He felt a twinge of compassion. He was proud that she had a father that she cared about.

"Is your mother coming to meet your teacher tonight?"

"I dunno—she knows my letter was stolen. She's s'posed to come to the Christmas program."

"Are you participating?"

"Yes sir. I sing with the choir."

"Good! Good Carletta, I believe that your letter, even though it's missing, I believe it's in good hands. I'm sure it will reach Santa Claus. Believe me; I think it will reach the right people."

"What 'cha mean? Is it going to the store?"

"I CAN'T SAY, Carletta. I just know that good things can happen. Ok, so just think positive and plan for the Christmas program."

Mr. Wallace signed Carletta's hall pass and sent her back to class. She and the other students had to practice their Christmas carols. After Carletta left, Mr. Wallace asked the secretary to try to reach the commander of a local army recruiting center. He also asked her to get the number to a local T.V. station.

When Carletta's mother came home, she found Carletta happier than she'd been for a week.

Mr. Wallace called me to the office."

"What did you do? Have you been fighting?"

"No. He talked to me about my letter."

"Did he have your letter?"

"I DON'T KNOW. He didn't say, but he did say that my letter is in good hands. I didn't really know what he meant by that."

"How did he get your letter—if he really had it?"

"I don't know. He wanted us to come to the Christmas program. You are going, aren't you, Mom? You know that I got to sing?"

"Yes. You know I want to see and hear you sing."

The excitement of the Christmas program was felt throughout the audience. Parents, with children in the program, were escorted by the art teacher into the multi-purpose room. They rushed to get the best seat available.

When the time came for the program to start, parents were informed by Mr. Wallace that there would be a special event taking place after the program was over. He encouraged them to stay for the event. "This is a special event that relates to a special class activity, so please be kind enough and share this unique event with us."

While he spoke, the different groups were being positioned on and off the stage by the music teacher and the teachers assisting her. The first part of the program opened with the short skit, titled "How Santa Gets Help."

After that presentation, two Christmas poems were recited by the second grade students. Following that, a short choral reading was presented. The musical part of the program was staged with a winter land background provided by the art teacher.

The choirs sang three songs; two popular Christmas songs and one Spiritual. The parents applauded, and the students took their bow.

The music teacher complimented the pupils. She thanked the parents for their support. She wished all a joy-filled holiday season and turned the program over to Mr. Wallace, the principal.

Mr. Wallace greeted the parents warmly. He complimented the pupils on their performances. While he was speaking, a man dressed in an army uniform rolled a TV monitor to the front of the room. He plugged the cord into the outlet.

"What I'm about to do is not the usual presentation. As you know, we have a lot of family members who have relatives in the Armed Services that are stationed abroad. They are not able to enjoy the holidays the way we are, and we are not able to share the holiday in any personal way unless we can mail or call them.

He stopped for a brief moment and turned to the man standing by the TV monitor. "This is Sgt. Larry Thompson, United States Army." The Sergeant nodded to the audience.

"Good evening." He spoke.

"Sergeant Thompson has worked with me to bring about a special event. This grew out of a situation that developed in Miss Carter's third grade class. Her class wrote letters to Santa a few weeks ago. While most requested toys, clothing, and games, one particular student expressed to Santa that she was concerned for her father. Some how, through some mysterious means of delivery, her letter ended up in my office. I found her request heart warming, and because of our technological advancements, I felt her request could be met. Thanks to Sergeant Thompson and our local TV station, her request was granted.

It's only fair that I say the letter belonged to our own Carletta Hill. So, I want Mrs. Hill and Carletta to understand that I was touched by Carletta's request. I hope that what you view will be both a present and a source of comfort. This tape will be yours to keep. It is a response to Carletta's request, which I hope you won't mind sharing with us. Sergeant Thompson, put the videotape in."

In a few seconds, a tall bronze soldier clad in army fatigues, stood and smiled.

"Hello, Carletta. I got a copy of your letter. It made me very happy. I miss you and your mother. I am well, and I hope to be able to come home soon. Stay in school, and do your best. Have a Merry Christmas and Happy New Year. I love you both, Dad."

Throughout the viewing, Carletta and her mother sat spellbound, speechless, and filled with joy. When the video ended, the Sergeant removed the tape, walked over to Mrs. Hill and handed her the video. He stretched out his hand and asked them to join him and Mr. Wallace at the front. All eyes were on Carletta and her mother.

Mrs. Hill had tears in her eyes; so did Carletta. As they were escorted to the front, Carletta thought, "My dad got my letter!" Immediately, Carletta hugged Mr. Wallace. Her mother thanked him and the Sergeant.

"Mrs. Hill, the tape is yours."

"Oh, thank you! This makes us very happy, and the Christmas will be a happy one!"

"Oh, I know what happened to my letter." Carletta said. "I bet Miss Carter gave it to Mr. Wallace. Did she, Mr. Wallace?"

"No-o, Carletta. One of your friends delivered it to one of Santa's helpers."

"Who is that?"

"Santa has helpers in all places, Carletta, so enjoy the gift. This tape is your Christmas gift."

"Thank you, but I sure wish I knew who stole my letter."

Mr. Wallace thought about the fingerprints on the letter, and then replied, "Just remember, Carletta, Santa has a lot of helpers."

Epilogue

The students and their parents left the auditorium. All were happy and pleased with the program. Many were congratulating Carletta and her mother. But none was as relieved as Marvin . . .

He was headed to the pencil sharpener when Carletta left her seat to line up for the fire drill. He saw her letter fall to the floor as her sweater was dragged across her desk. He picked it up and joined the line of students outside the class.

He was folding it when a teacher looked at him and told him to put it away. He didn't want the paper to be seen in his hands so he slipped it into Joey's coat pocket.

Marvin wasn't really thinking when he folded the paper and slipped it into Joey's coat pocket as they walked single file out of the building. He just knew that he didn't want a teacher to see him with something in his hands. He was really happy now but couldn't figure out how Mr. Wallace got the letter. Maybe Joey gave it to the principal. Maybe Joey was the helper. He also felt good because the letter was never stolen—it just traveled until Santa got it.